PRAISE FOR
THE MASTERPIECE

…*"Very easy to read, lovely small words."*

S. Dumba [starlette]

…*"This work reminds me of a young Brendan Behan, a drunken Behan, but a Behan all the same. This insightful work should be on the Leaving Cert. Syllabus."*

T. Murphy [professor]

…*"I've read it three times, it just gets better and better."*

B. Twomey [housewife]

…*"The pages felt lovely and smooth…unmissable."*

S. Wonder [singer]

GW00707587

... *"Coo coo coo."*

[pigeon]

... *"A ruler can be used for many other pleasures besides cutting pages."*

C. O'Sullivan [mistress]

... *"The best part for me was not paying for it."*

R. Wyder [actor]

... *"It's a weapon of mass destruction, it must be blown up."*

G. Bush [madman]

THE MASTERPIECE uncut

THE
MASTERPIECE uncut

Alan Shortt

MERLIN
PUBLISHING

Published in 2002 by
Merlin Publishing
16 Upper Pembroke Street
Dublin 2
Ireland
Tel: + 353 1 6764373
Fax: + 353 1 6764368
publishing@merlin.ie
www.merlin-publishing.com

British Library Cataloguing in Publication Data
A catalogue record for this book is available from the British Library

ISBN 1-903582-46-6

5 4 3 2 1

Typeset by Gough Typesetting Services
Cover design by Pierce Design
Cover photograph by Susan Jefferies
Printed by Colour Books Ltd., Dublin

Dedication

I'd like to dedicate this book to my son, Sam, especially for inspiration in chapter 18. Also to my wife and lover, Colette, thanks for all the cups of coffee and constant interruptions which helped with the artistic style of my first novel. And finally to all the people who actually paid hard-earned money to buy this book ... I'd like to say thank you.

Preface

I got the idea for this book while sitting on the toilet. It had a nice wooden seat. Now normally wooden seats aren't the best, because if there's a lot of men in the house, the little bits that get away and stay on the seat [cause men never wipe the seat after them] the little stray drips begin to stain and corrode the wood, leaving very ugly reminders of previous little accidents, which reminds me, I must replace it with a plastic seat. As I sat there I said to myself, why don't I write a book, everybody else has so why can't I! It's true what they say "There's one inside everyone." So here we go and I hope you enjoy it. To read this book you will need a lot of patience, solitude, and a huge imagination. You will also need a scissors or a knife of some sort, so you may need a grown-up to help you.

... my Editor was just on the phone, in fact she's always on the phone recently, she rings me more often than my bank manager. Things must be bad, or else my bank manager is on a career break. She's wondering how the book is going. "Great," I said, "nearly there!" Little does she know that I've just started it. I told her that my computer got a virus and died, so she's extended my deadline ... Thank God for that ...

Survival Kit – How to Survive this Book

Please read carefully before proceeding. For safety reasons please don't skip this page. For the sake of your own health and the health of your family, please read these instructions.

… I'm sure you're the sort of person who knows everything about everything and never reads instructions, you're the sort of person that when you get a flat pack washing machine, you just whip out your screwdriver and start screwing for Ireland, and four frustrated hours later you end up with a lawnmower with a glass door that spin-dries your lawn at 65 degrees!

So I urge you … please put down the screwdriver and read the instructions. Please put it down now and walk away! … Well done … now take a deep breath, and go and put on the kettle … I take my tea with two sugars and one milk.

In order to get full family enjoyment from this book you will need the following tools by your side at all times. [You can share if you like but the desire to share might lead to a divorce or a short-term separation, and it really sounds silly telling your friends that you broke up over who was going to have the whisk first also when you divorce you'll find you only have half the friends you used to have, your half, unless some of them liked your partner more than they like you, which can happen if you're not a nice person, so you may need help, and you could visit a psychiatrist *see page 7.*]

Sorry, the sun is shining, got to get out of here, I'll give you the instructions when I get back …

Ten minutes later

... oh that felt great. My apologies about that rude exit, but you know yourself, when the sun shines in Ireland you've got to make the most of it, there's only so many vitamin D tablets you can take. I believe that one day soon the weather man will have a satellite so powerful that he will be able to tell us what day in the year will have brilliant sunshine from sunrise to sunset and they will make that day a public holiday.

So where was I ... oh yes ... what you will need to read this book is:

A ruler

A scissors

[Please get an adult or a young, good-looking blonde trainee hairdresser to help you with this, because scissors can be dangerous in the wrong hands when you don't know how to use them.]

A pair of binoculars

A magnifying glass

A whisk

An imagination

[If you're an accountant or a solicitor you can borrow one of these from a friend, then again you don't have any friends so you might as well stop reading now and go and do something useful ... like ... go and count your Communion money and put the kettle on again ... I take my tea with two sugars and one milk.]

4 egg whites

4 oz of caster sugar

4 oz of icing sugar

2 teaspoons of cornflour

1 teaspoon of white vinegar

A pinch of salt

8 fl oz of cream

One *Cadbury's Flake*

Strawberries and kiwi fruit to decorate

Electric beater

A baking tray

A sieve

Some parchment paper

An oven

A hammer

A rubber spatula

A bottle of wine

A compass and a good sense of direction. If you're a man stop now and ask for directions, or ask a woman because you're probably going to get frustrated and start shouting at somebody.

... my Editor has been on again. I'm thinking of changing my number. I told her, my pet tortoise got a virus and died. She's extended the deadline again ... So I'd better start stealing ideas from... Sorry I mean writing some original stuff!

CHAPTER ONE

The Horse

When you're driving behind a horse-box at thirty-six miles an hour in a sixty mile an hour zone, looking at a horse's arse for miles upon end, did you ever wonder … hmmmmm … why do horses always face forward in horse-boxes? Are they addicted to exhaust fumes? Maybe it's the only way the farmer has of getting them into, what is to the horse, a glorified wardrobe on wheels. First the farmer starts the jeep, revs up the engine, gets a big black cloud out of the exhaust, opens the box door and says, "There's a good horsey, get a good sniff of that, cause I know what you like to sniff, come on now horsey, suck them fumes, baby!" Maybe the exhaust fumes keep him calm, maybe the farmer doesn't want the horse to see where he's going, and that way he won't be able to find his way home, unless of course he was "Black Beauty" who could find his way home quicker than a champion racer pigeon who'd only been left off from next door. Also, when they do their toilet, they have to walk backwards over it when they exit the box, and the smell up the front must be terrible … phewww … then again they're so high on exhaust fumes they don't mind walking in their own sh*t. Surely the horse would prefer to stick his head out the back of the box, fresh air, his s*** to his back, and a chance to spot the odd good-looking piebald pony … "Pwlpwlpwlpwlpwl … will you look at that fine filly, young free and single, not a saddle in sight … Pwlpwlpwlpwl … look at the fetlocks on her, and them lips sucking the grass like spaghetti, I'd say she'd take candy from a baby, hmmm I wish I was a baby! … pwlpwlpwlpwl … wouldn't mind sinking my teeth into her mane … pwlpwlpwlpwl …can't beat a good bit of rough piebaldy … pwlpwlpwlpwl-pwlpwlpwlpwlpwl!" [That's the sound a horny horse makes when he sees a piebald on the side of the road] …

IF

... Stevie Bolger rang again. "What about a game of golf" he said in his mid-Atlantic DJ tones. You may remember Stevie from such shows as Stevie Bolger Live, Stevie Recorded as Live *[because he was on holidays in Malta] and* Stevie 2.45 Live. *"No. I can't play golf today, I'm still working on the book," I said. "Jesus, you're forever working on that bloody book, what is it? ... some kind of masterpiece or something?" "Would you shish awhile," I whispered. "My editor might be listening, she's resorted to hanging around the house ... but thanks for the idea for the name, that's a start ... bye now" and I hung up. I opened up the front door and banged it loudly, then quietly I snuck into the downstairs toilet. My editor, thinking I'd left the building, ran to the front door, opened it and left, crawling on all fours like a sniffer dog, just in case she might be spotted. I think I'll change the locks ...*

... Writing acts like a sort of release – it calms the senses, and unblocks the mind, and allows you get rid of all that pent-up nonsense you have in your head, so you can make way for a load of new nonsense to take its place. Why don't you try it? Sit at your computer, place your hands on your keyboard ... take a deep breath ... and ... let go! ... I'll bet you never knew how much rubbish was in there!

1. Eskimos use fridges to keep food from freezing.

CHAPTER TWO

The Psychiatrist

Mary hadn't been feeling well for a while, she'd lost her sex drive, her energy, her sense of humour, and her left ear in a door-jamb accident at work. Her friends said it was quite common to have a shrink….

"Everyone has one," said Angela, "even the lady in number 10 got one for her dog. Apparently the Jack Russell is a schizo, poor little thing thinks it's George the St Bernard from the movie …"

"I never shop there!" Mary said, quite indignantly. Her hearing wasn't the same after the accident. "It keeps digging up dead people in the graveyard. I suppose the little devil thinks they've been killed in some sort of avalanche."

Angela chuckled …

Did Mary go to the shrink, was the dog a closet necrophiliac, see page 124 to find out! And if you don't want to or you can't find it, that's okay too.

YOU

2. The sentence "the quick brown fox jumps over the lazy dog" uses every letter in the alphabet.

3. Dolphins sleep with one eye open.

Auntie Pauline's Dip in the Nip

You will need:
> *Philadelphia* cheese
> Soured cream
> 4 cloves of garlic
> 2 avocados
> 4 tomatoes
> 2 scallions
> 1 jar of taco sauce
> Grated cheese.

Serving dish approx. 3 inches deep or what ever looks posh in your press.

This is a four layered dip to be eaten with nachos. It's best eaten naked, because it can be quite messy, so when you drop a bit, its much more fun to lick it off.

First mix an equal amount of *Philadelphia* cheese and soured cream together. Add the chopped garlic – this is your first layer, spread this in your serving dish. For the second layer, peel the avocado and remove the seed and throw them into your next door neighbour's garden. Chop the peeled avocado, tomatoes, and scallions in to small pieces and spread, gently over your first layer. Do this with your fingers – it's much more sensuous. Then pour the jar of mild taco sauce over that layer. Sprinkle with grated cheese and vwolla – The Dip!

Turn on the heating. Get naked (shoulders back, this will make you look less saggy). Then, take a nacho and slowly, sink it deep into the dip, and scoop up a dollop. Push it into your partner's mouth, making sure a little bit oozes out of his or her mouth, and drips onto their body ... mmm ... mmmm ... then lick it off!

Have the ice cream on stand by just in case!

4. A duck's quack doesn't echo, and nobody knows why, especially the ducks. It drives them quacked!

CAN'T

5. More people use blue toothbrushes than red ones.

6. The bible has been translated into klingon.

CHAPTER THREE

The Wig Men

They could hear the waves crashing against the cliffs, millions of gallons of salt water pounding the rocks at 200 miles per hour, the hurricane wind whipping up the sea foam high above the cliffs, falling like an alpine blizzard onto the lonely white thatched cottage.

A lone candle flickered in the corner, their last candle. They had been stranded for two weeks and four days. John was a librarian, Michael was a tax accountant, and Brian was a professional altar boy, very popular amongst the clergy. They all had one thing in common: they all wore a toupee, badly! John's was a sort of sandy colour, cut straight at the back but too short to cover his grey sidelocks. Michael's was a shiny jet-black *Oasis* style, he thought the greasy shine made it look more authentic, and Brian's was fiery red and curled up at the ends [it had been handed down through his family of crown toppers for centuries, which meant it didn't fit very well, so he would always shake dusty cereal on his suits in the hope that people would be distracted by the mountains of fake dandruff covering his shoulders.]

John stood on the rickety table balancing on his one good leg – he had burnt the other one while drying his socks on the candle – and held the little hand-radio as high as he could, turning it back and forth to get a signal. Suddenly through a cloud of static ...

"And now the sea area forecast for the next week," said the announcer, "hurricane winds force 10 gusting to force 12 in all areas ..."

John looked at Michael and said "We won't be going out today." "No, John ... we won't!"

READ

7. You can lead a cow upstairs but you can't lead him downstairs.

… oops I just got an idea …oh that really hurt, I'd better go get a head massage …

THIS

The Meeting

The meeting of the Northside Hounds Club was brought to order. All the sweaty beer-bellied men sat around the wall. It resembled a gay *ceilí* in the west of Ireland – all the butch men on one side of the room and the camp men on the other. When the Mary Ring band started, one of them had to be brave enough to place his warm drink on the ground under the chair, stand up, rearrange his meat and two veg, *[the jeans were very tight, millions of innocent sperm were murdered at every sitting]* and walk across the divide, the no-man's land, the long mile, the huge empty maple floor *[which was covered in salt to make it more slidey, oh how they loved to slide]*, and ask a man to dance.

"Love the shirt, would you like to face me for this, miss?" he asked nervously.

"No," came the answer, echoing around the room like a scream in a Mitchelstown cave. Mary Ring stopped squeezing her box, the room fell silent, you could hear a fly fart.

"I'd prefer your friend!" he winked.

"Well, I don't mind if you don't. You know what they say, two is company and three is fifty quid."

"Deal!" He spat on his hand and they shook on it. Mary Ring's squeeze box started up *The Siege of Venice* and they flung each other around the room till drops of sweat had been squeezed out of their tight jeans, not a live sperm between them.

But there were no gay men in the Northside Hounds Club, they figured gay men didn't like hounds, they preferred poodles, that's what the hounds eat for breakfast – pretty, white, tasty poodles.

Jack, the president, had been shopping for a new stud hound in England, and he had managed to smuggle it home in the boot of his car. Two days and three nights and a gale force sea-crossing, and a dog with no sea-legs. You can imagine the state of Jack's car, never mind the state of the dog. At least Jack was able to shower the dog while the wife was at the bingo, and the car, well … he drove it into the river and reported it stolen. Jack would do anything for the Northside Hounds Club.

Jack hoisted the new hound up onto the table. There was a unified sharp intake of breath followed by a chorus of burps. They had never seen such a fine hound in the club since their last sire, Getitupquick, eloped with a local bitch who was in heat the previous year. They had placed wanted ads all over the local area … "Have You Seen This Dog". They got loads of false "leads" *[no pun intended … then again….]* most of them from deserted husbands saying, "He's shagging my wife and you know he can have her!"

All the club members admired their new prize hound.

"Hasn't he got powerful ears, long ears are a great sign in a hound," remarked Johnny.

"Look at his shoulders, they're as straight as a poker," said Mikey.

"Hasn't he got a fine wet nose," said Peter, slightly salivating.

Then from the corner of the room, Fergus *[or Gussey as he was called]*, stood up, shook the dandruff from his shoulders, slowly approached the hound – everybody was in awe of this momentous occasion, because Gussey hadn't spoken a word since Getitupquick had disappeared. That was seven months ago. He was very close to that hound, some would say too close. Suddenly, Gussey took a deep breath, and said …

"Come here, lads …hasn't he a powerful pair of balls!"

… I treat my body like a temple … Temple Bar!

...Stevie rang me again. I wish he'd get a job, or better again, get me a job, cause this book thing, is too hard. It's making my head hurt.

"How about I bring my putting machine out to your house, and we can practice on your carpet" suggested Stevie.

"Sorry ..." I said, "I won't be able to do that."

"Oh come on Al, all work and no play makes Alan a very rich man!" he laughed.

"That's the whole problem," I said, "we're not rich at all. We had to sell the carpet to pay for food!"

"Oh I'll leave you alone then, bye!" he hung up.

The phone rang again. "Hello," I said. It was Stevie again...

"Yah ... Al, I was just thinking, let me know when your selling your golf clubs, I'll give you a fair price!" said Stevie.

I hung up. This bloody book better sell!

8. A giraffe can clean its ears with its tongue ... Hmmm ... lovely taste of ear wax.

YOU

.... my Editor rang again, Jesus there must be nobody else writing books this month. I wouldn't mind but she's not even paying me, then again would you blame them. What do you think? You're reading it ... so listen ... if you think I should be paid for this, write a letter to the publishers [their address is somewhere here in the book I think] and tell them how much I should be paid... thanks a million... that's a hint ...

… if you can read this then you don't need glasses!

SHOULD

CHAPTER FOUR

THE STREET

Okay here we go, the pain in my head has gone and I'm ready to write …

The street was dark, pitch black, you couldn't see a damn thing. It was so dark the cats were banging into each other. 'Meow …ow! …Meow …ow! Meow … ow! Meow…'
    Even the …ah …hmmm …even the …

Oh …look …this is going nowhere. You can try and finish it if you want. Let me know how you get on by e-mailing me care of publishing@merlin.ie

…this writing lark is much harder than I thought.

9. 35% of people who use personal ads for dating are already married.

10. There were no ponies in the pony express, there were just horses.

GRAB

Sporting Autobiography

[ghostwritten by K Reane, so you'll have to excuse the spelling]

I remember I was working in a pub in Kerry at the time, and the local football team would regularly frequent the pub and stay until very late, normally till 3 in the morning, unless they had an important match the following day, then they'd leave at half past 2 in the morning. As the weeks went by I began to build up a friendship with the trainer, Mikey Daly, a big mountainy man with hands like shovels. He had a big long wisp of brown dyed hair combed from his left ear all the way over the top of his head to his right ear, in a vain attempt to cover his bald patch, and on a windy day, the long wispy mane would take flight and land on his left shoulder. Mikey would spit on his hand and would firmly rub the hair back into place. His nickname locally was "Trapper John MD", because of his initials **M**ikey **D**aly. I told him I had played for Cork at minor level [a slight exaggeration] but I was after seven pints of stout. I could easily have boasted that I played GAA for Ireland!

"Would you like to play for us tomorrow, it's the final of the shield and we're one man short," Mikey enquired. I was chuffed to be asked, and it would definitely beat counting scones in the kitchen [Sunday was always the chef's scone stocktaking day].

"Jesus, I'd love to play Mikey, thanks a million for asking," as I jumped behind the bar to pull our 8th illegal pint.

"But I've no gear with me, no boots, no togs, no socks, no nothing!" I said.

"No problem there boyeen, the fella you're replacing is about your size, maybe a little taller, a bit broader around the shoulders, but the main thing is that you're the spitting image of him." So God made a taller version of me in Kerry, just great, I thought. Mikey continued his slur …

"I'm sure we can ask his mother in the morning for his gear, I'm sure he didn't bring it to where he's gone."

"Christ Mikey, don't tell me he died?" I said worryingly.

"Christ no, boyeen, he's gone to America," laughed Mikey, his hearty laugh always came from the bottom of his lungs, and was normally followed by a fit of coughing resulting in a great big lump of green cigarette phlegm being deposited into his crusty hanky. You'd never see Mikey in the pub on a Wednesday, cause that was hanky boiling day!

The Jahova's Witnesses just called at the door. I said we just had our windows cleaned last week. They weren't amused, I think all they wanted was a cup of tea and a sneaky look at Sky News. But I did ask them how to spell jahova, cause I'd give them a mention in the book, and they told me ... Jehovah! A day doesn't go by without some fecker calling at the door, now I know why housewives don't get anything done during the day.

11. A crocodile can't stick its tongue out.

How To Become A Star

'...well to be honest, all I did was sat around all day doing nothing ...sometimes I'd talk to the chickens, and sometimes I wouldn't. Then at night I'd get drunk and jump in the pool, sometimes I'd take all my clothes off, and sometimes I wouldn't. Then I'd get up the next afternoon, late, and start all over again. It was really very boring....'

A talentless Big Brother Contestant.

THE

CHAPTER FIVE

It was a typical autumn day, the leaves were falling off the trees, flowing down the gullies, blocking up the drains. This was the boom time for the contract drain cleaners, who spend most of their summer unblocking tourist town sewers which can't cope with the sudden explosion of tampon and condom flushing tourists – they'd flush their dead rabbit down the toilet if they thought it would fit down the U bend … then again with a little push with the toilet brush it just might. Charlie was a 32-year-old engineer who loved drains …

I've got to go cut the grass. If you prefer Sci-fi turn to page 89.

12. Ants always fall over on their right side when they're drunk.

The
Actor

... then the phone stopped ringing.

BINOCULARS

13. A snail can sleep for 3 years.

14. Butterflies taste with their feet.

... at the moment I'm sitting here with one of them slender tone thingy-me-bobs strapped to my stomach, because the man on the shopping channel says it's better than going to the gym. So here I am, getting electric shocks every two seconds, my hair standing on end. All it seems to be doing is firming up my fat. I reckon if you have a layer of blubber like most of us have, then these things are useless – you use it Christmas Day, then the batteries go out, and it gets thrown in the hot press with the beer making kit. Anyway, who wants to have a firm chest like those vein-popping bodybuilders on TV. I don't want to have two giant breasts, because then I wouldn't be able to fly or climb Mount Everest, because they'd explode.

... BANG! ... SPLAT! ... THE END!

Colette's Fishy Dishy

You will need:
1 side of smoked salmon
4 medium potatoes
Grated cheese
1 tub of light cream
1 glass of wine
1 quiche dish

First take a sip of wine, mmm ...mmm, tastes like more? Then peel your potatoes and boil them until they're cooked, leave them cool a little. Then slice them into potato type slices. Arrange a layer of sliced potatoes in your dish, then a layer of smoked salmon, then another layer of potatoes, then another layer of smoked salmon, then another layer of potatoes. Now pour the tub of cream over the whole lot and sprinkle the top with a generous helping of grated cheese. Pop into a medium oven [160ºC] for 20/25 minutes until cheese is golden. Alternatively you can place it under a hot grill for a few minutes to give the cheese an extra crunch, while the fishy dishy is cooking, polish off the glass of wine.

Serve immediately, with a simple green on the side.

Serving suggestion:

Put on the heating and wear nothing but an apron and a smile... Enjoyyyyyyy...

NOW

CHAPTER SIX

The Match

It was a cold breezy Sunday, and we all piled out of Mass. You could feel the excitement in the air, Valley Rovers versus Erin Rangers. There was going to be blood. We togged off at the side of the road, because there were no dressing-rooms in those days – you were lucky to have a pitch free of blue rinse sheep. Mikey handed me a plastic bag.

"What size boots are you, boyeen?"

"Nine!" I said, quite proudly. You know what they say, big feet, big … shoes. "Young Johnny was size ten, so they'll have to do, maybe if you stuffed some newspaper into the toe of the shoe, it might make them more comfortable," he said, ripping apart the *Sunday World*.

There's a knack to togging off on the side of the road, especially when you're being eyed up and down by the crowds making their way from the Mass to the match. First you remove your shirt and quickly put on the jersey, which turned out to be two sizes too big; you untie both shoes so they're easy to slip out of, then you drop your trousers [your vanity being shielded by the extra long jersey] step in and out of each shoe, quickly removing your trousers and pulling up your togs, which looked like a pair of plus fours, then double lace the *Sunday World*-stuffed boots. The smell of Deepheat filled the air as we ran onto the pitch.

"Go on, Johnny, give 'em hell," Mikey roared. What's he saying, I thought, my name isn't Johnny. "You are a fair man, Johnny," said Tony, the captain, followed by a broad wink. Then it clicked. I was an illegal player, playing under an assumed name, in a kit two sizes too big for me. The man I was marking was a bit of a mammy's boy. He had the 'flu, constantly sneezing and spluttering, and any time the ball would go dead his mother ran on the pitch to blow his nose for him. "There you go, son, give it a good blow," she said, wiping his snotty nose, "you lost a bit of weight in America, Johnny. You'd want to be eating some more of them McDougals," she remarked. I'm sure she meant something else. I just nodded and pretended to tie my doubled lace boot. It wasn't long before I realised why I wasn't getting any ball, because the team kept shouting "Here Johnny, take the ball, Johnny, run Johnny, go Johnny, go Johnny, go go go!" and I'd just stand there looking around, looking like a feckin' eejit, but it wasn't long before I got into it, running, passing, a quick solo of the ball, and the odd "God bless you" every time my man sneezed.

It was in the middle of the second half when things began to get dirty. My belly was full of orange segments from the half-time team talk, and my jersey was covered in snot – not my snot but my opponent's snot – and to make things worse, every time I tackled him hard, his mother would run on the pitch waving a hanky saying "Yera Johnny, would you go easy on him, can't you see he has the 'flu!" Like a bull to a red rag, the next high ball that came down our way, *[the next bit happened in slow motion, like a bad episode of the* A-Team*]* we both jumped high into the air, I elbowed his chin, there was a cloud of snot, we landed, hard, with my size ten boot intentionally dug deep into his shin bone. There was a loud deafening crack, followed by a scream of pain, then all hell broke loose. His mother ran onto the pitch, but this time she had an umbrella, a big, old, black umbrella with a long metal spike at the end of it.

"Johnny! You bastard!" she screamed. "Didn't I tell you to go easy on him, you're just like your father, a dirty rotten bastard."

She didn't even know my father. Oh yes I forgot, I'm not me, I'm Johnny and I'd better duck, quick! She swung the umbrella like a three iron, I ducked, the referee got it right against the ear, blood spattered everywhere,

"Oh Jesus! … Father, I'm sorry!" The referee was the parish priest. "It was meant for that bastard … sorry, I mean that…

that … American Johnny!" she squealed.

"Run Johnny!" shouted Mikey, with his wispy mane blowing in the wind. "Get the feck out of there, run for your life."

Johnny got a three match ban, the parish priest lost an ear, and he had to swap sides in the confessional, mother and son went to America to track down Johnny, and were never seen again, and me, well this is my first time admitting to the intentional foul that ended a very promising footballing career. This might help to sell the book!

*Please serialize this bit in **The Sunday Times**, or **Beano**, I don't care which.*

15. Chewing gum while peeling onions will stop you crying.

16. Elephants can't jump.

My friend (yes I have a friend, are we surprised?) just came back from holidays,

"...ooohhhh the place was gorgeous, the sun, the sand, the cereal, it was so crunchy, and it was so cheap, I met up with this gang from the North, of course they got there for half the price we paid – you know yourself – but they were a hoot, you would have loved them, we spent the whole time together, at night we'd all eat together, did I tell you how cheap it was?, well listen here, a meal for the eleven of us only cost FOUR EURO AND SIXTY-SEVEN CENT and included buckets of wine, starters, main courses, the whole shebang! and there was mountains of food, I came home with more money than I left with, oh you'd love it, next time you'll have to come too, oh and did I tell you that we're all meeting up for a reunion next month, to swap photographs and things, we're thinking of making it a beach party, did I tell you how cheap it was over there, the beer was for nothing, you could easily buy a house for a quarter of the price over here, oh it was so beautiful, and so cheap..."

She eventually took a breath ...

"Well why don't you go and live there then you silly cow!" I roared.

I feel a doggy poem coming on ... hmmm. Let's see ... ah yes ...

The doggies held a conference,
They came from near and far,
Some came by aeroplane,
And some by motor car.

As each doggy queued,
To sign the visitors book,
Each doggy took his arsehole off
And hung it on a hook.

As they were assembled,
Each purebred dam and sire,
Some dirty rotten doggy,
Came in and shouted "fire!"

The doggies were in a panic
They had no time to look,
So each doggy grabbed an arsehole
Off the nearest hook.

And that is why you'll see today,
A **dog** will leave a bone,
To sniff another's **arsehole**,
To see if its his own!

17. If Barbie was life-size, her measurements would be 39-23-33, and she'd stand seven feet two inches tall, and she'd be made of plastic and have no brain ... Hmmm ... remind you of anybody?

THE ONION

A post-modernist poem to make you cry.

Get an onion and peel it,
(Are you crying yet?)
Cut both ends off the onion,
(Are you crying yet?)
Cut the onion into pieces,
(Are you crying yet?)
Place your eyes close to the chopped onions
(Are you crying yet?)
Now open a press and close it hard on your finger
...
(If you're not crying by now, you are probably dead!
Or just in severe pain!)

Onion suggestions: wear swimming goggles while cutting onions – this will stop you crying.

SUGGEST

CHAPTER FIVE

Continued …

It was a typical autumn day in the year 2080. The last living leaf fell of the tree, flowed down the gully and into the drain. This was the boom time for the contract drain cleaners, who spent most of their summer unblocking tourist town sewers which couldn't cope with the sudden explosion of microchip, tampon and condom flushing tourists – they'd flush their dead rabbit down the toilet if they thought it would fit down the U-bend … [they could never design a toilet without a U-bend not even in the future] then again with a little push with the toilet zapper it just might. 110-year-old Charlie loved drains …

Finish it yourself if you like …I couldn't be bothered.

19. No word in English rhymes with month.

18. All polar bears are left-handed.

... you may be wondering by now, "why all the blank pages?", well, it's to give your eyes a break, reading can be very tiring, they're also very handy for you to make notes as you go along, or maybe you forgot to do the shopping and need to make a list. Use a blank page, then you can bring the book to the shop and read while you shop. But I find the best use for all the blank pages is when you're sitting on the toilet, because let's face it everybody reads while sitting on the toilet (except for women, they just hover) and you've just realized there's no toilet paper left. This book has many uses!

YOU

CHAPTER EIGHT

The Book – At Last

I could feel water lapping against my cheek. My head hurt. I opened my eyes, it was dusk, there were rocks, trees, and water. I lifted my head slowly out of the water, and dragged myself up the beach. I could hear wolves in the trees, howling, growling, barking, it sent shivers down my spine. I passed out again.

[In fact they weren't wolves at all, there was a local bitch in heat, and the dogs of the area had all gathered for their monthly gang bang or dog bang. The bitch stood in the centre, keeping order, she decided which dog, which way, and when. Nearly all of the dogs went for the doggy style position, except for one, the big Northsider hound, he wanted to do it man style. Uhhh, how she loved something kinky. Then there was the little mongrel terrier who was on the small side. He stood on a log, balancing on two legs while the bitch backed up slowly. The dogs went at it like hammer and tongs, some dogs going twice – cause they could, little did they know that the vet had put her on the pill. This was only pure pleasure for her, she wasn't going to have their mongrel shaggy puppies, oh no, she was going to save her womb for a purebred, an out-of-towner …]

I woke up to the sound of rustling and whining, a dog was shagging my leg.

"Get off!" I shouted. The dog looked up at me with its big brown droopy eyes and gave me that little puppy-dog look.

"Okay, just one more time, but don't expect me to cook breakfast," I whispered. He gave me a big wet lick on the face. Attached to my leg was a rope. Why it was there, how it got there, who put it there, was a complete mystery to me. I felt terrible – my head was spinning, my stomach was woozy and my chest hurt. I must have broken a rib while coughing up the lake.

I decided I'd better dry off and get some shelter for the

night. I gathered some logs, got two dry sticks and vigorously rubbed them together. It wasn't long before I had a big roaring fire – who says you don't learn anything from reality TV. Then myself and Frisky (that's what I christened the dog), cuddled up for the night. God, how he snored.

Yet another licking woke me in the morning. Frisky's breath stank of putrid dog food. His tail wagging, all excited he was and to show his gratitude, he had a dead rabbit waiting by my feet,

"Typical, first you shag me and now you want breakfast," I said, as I skinned the rabbit, badly. Various memories flashed through my brain – falling into water, sinking fast, gasping for breath, bubbles rising to the surface, sinking sinking …

"Jesus Christ!" I shouted, dropping the half-skinned rabbit onto the fire. My brain was overloading with violent images. Driving home from work, a truck crashed into me on my left hand side, my head smashed against the steering wheel, I was pulled out of the car, blood streaming into my eyes, all I could see were the lights of the truck, two men shouting at me …

"Right, you bastard, keep your mouth shut and you won't be harmed." They shoved me into the back of their truck, and sped away. They tied a rope onto my leg, the truck jerked violently on the road. It wasn't long before we came to a sudden stop. There was a screech of tyres as they backed up the truck and the back doors swung open. All I could see was the moon reflecting on the water. One of them picked up the block that was attached to the rope and said in a broad Dublin accent …

"I hope your middle name is Houdini!"

They both grabbed me and threw me out, falling, falling, falling, splashing into the cold dark lake, first me, then the block. Obviously they weren't very good at tying knots, because the block must have come free while I was unconscious, and then I floated to the beach. Why would someone want to kill me? I'm just a sausage salesmen. Maybe that's why Frisky likes me so much. I know I wasn't very popular in school, but nobody can a hold a grudge for that long. I stole Timmy Sullivan's girlfriend when I was in college, but as it turned out he didn't like her very much, in fact we're still friends. We bought a life policy from him last month, joint cover on myself and my wife for one million euro. Now that I'm dead she's a millionaire. But she wouldn't want me dead. We were childhood sweethearts, she doesn't have a bad bone in her body.

BOOK

20. Rubber bands last longer when put in the fridge.

The problem with working from home is that people keep calling to your door; the amount of salesmen that call during the day is astounding. We live in a country where usually the whole household has to go out to work in order to pay for the mortgage, two cars, the dog, and one point two children. In fact, even the one point two children are sometimes sent to work, part time modelling and the odd bit of busking at lunch time. So if there's nobody at home why do salesmen persist in calling? Take this morning for instance. There were no cars in any of my neighbour's driveways[the one point two children use them to go busking] but he still called at every door. Maybe he thought that everybody hide their cars during the day, and just pretends they're at work, and when the door bell rings, they all run out the back door and into their shed and hide behind the giant bag of Peat Moss. Anyway, it was my turn. The door bell rang, there was nowhere to hide. I don't have a giant bag of Peat Moss and the neighbour's shed was bulging with refugees, so I slowly walked down the stairs and opened the door. A big smile crossed his face — at last a victim! He wore what looked like his Confirmation suit, all tidy and tight. He had a folder under his arm and a laminate hanging around his neck with his name, photograph and company logo. His name was John.

"Hello, my name is John," he said.

"And I don't want to buy anything," I said curtly.

"I'm wondering if you'd be interested in an alarm system," he said.

"I'm very sorry, but the dog is after getting sick all over the baby, and anyway I already have one, look at the box … up there … on the wall!"

Suddenly there was the sound of a dog barking [I

don't have a dog, it must have been on the TV.] *John got a terrible fright and began to speak quicker.* "Well how about I replace your alarm boxes with my company's boxes, just for advertising purposes."

"What's in it for me?" *The dog barked again, but still no sound of the baby. At this stage John was straining to look over my shoulder to see if there was any sign of life from the baby,*

"Well, how about a free service for your alarm," he replied worriedly. I thought for a moment [it really hurt I must stop this thinking lark it's just too painful.]

"No thanks! I'd better check the baby!" I said, and slammed the door. Why would he give me a free service for just letting him use his boxes on my wall. What advantage is it to him, free advertising. Nah ... if somebody wants an alarm, they look up the phone book, I'm sure they don't drive around housing estates looking up at alarm boxes on the wall and taking down phone numbers. "Oh look, darling, isn't that a lovely box there, I think that would really suit our colour scheme!" ... "Or what about that one there, great shape, great contours!" I don't think so, anyway you'd probably be arrested for stalking. Then I thought again ... ouch!

John was head of sales in a large multinational alarm company. He was useless at his job – his excuse for bad sales figures was that everybody had an alarm and those who didn't, had a dog. John was fired. He decided feck them, them and their corporate lingo, they know nothing about the real world, I'm better than them, I can be bigger than them. So John set up on his own. Before he left his old job he gained access to all the company records, and stole all the names and addresses of everyone who had bought an alarm from them during the last seven years. With his client base already in place, he drives around the country. It was a simple marketing plan. First he calls to the house offering a free service, and who turns down a free service? Nobody. Well, except me. He changes the box on the wall, and while he's doing the free service he disables the alarm. The next day, while the poor innocent people with new alarm boxes on the wall are out at work, or hiding behind a giant bag of Peat Moss in their shed, John breaks into the house, easy-peasy. He only steals cash, because nobody ever admits to having cash stolen – too many questions, where did you get it, have you any receipts, and they know it's silly having it in the house and everyone would say "I told you so!" He might also steal the odd pair of panties ... John likes panties, he loves the feel of panties, he uses them to polish his car, very soft, very smooth and they never fail to bring up a good shine on a black metallic finish.

The following day he calls to the house again asking if everything is okay.

"Hello, I'm John, and I'm just making sure your new boxes are okay."

The homeowners are too embarrassed to say they've been robbed of three grand in cash and two pairs of panties. They look at John and say,

"You know what, John, maybe you could install a new alarm for us, the one we had was really old and anyway, your box is already on the wall ..."

"No problemo!" says John with a big wry smile, "and you know what ... I'll even polish your car for free!"

21. Peanuts are one of the ingredients of dynamite.

22. A shark is the only fish that can blink with both eyes.

...my Editor just called at the door, I told her I had the whole book finished, but a terrible thing happened ...the dog ate it ...so she's taking the dog to the vet for an operation.

Worst thing is, I don't own a dog, so I borrowed my next door neighbour's Shitsu ...small dog ...big book ...sore belly!

The Dinner Party

"Oh S***!" she cried, as she dropped her large John Roches glass full of red wine on the new very expensive sheepskin rug.

An overwhelming silence descended upon the room. Everybody stopped breathing; a skinny model fainted due to lack of oxygen; but nobody cared, all eyes were on the sheepskin rug, as it soaked up the ruby red Premier cru. It was like a huge sheep sponge just lying there. You could hear the dead fibres gulping, gulping as they drank every last drop …

All the guests just stood there, except the model, staring, staring, at the fluffy, now soggy sheepskin rug, as it was slowly engulfed by the large red tide.

"That's the same colour my uncle uses to mark his sheep on the hills of Connemara. Well … maybe not as red, and now that I come to think of it … maybe not as big, but you could be certain sure, he could see his sheep from miles around," said Sean, nephew of a sheep farmer in the west of Ireland.

"I think it looks like your birth mark Sheila," shouted Cyril, Sheila's husband.

"No, that's purple," mused Tom, Sheila's lover.

Cyril didn't care about their affair, it meant he had more time to play golf and that suited him down to the ground. He had won the president's prize that morning. His new handicap was seven. He was chuffed.

"Quick throw some salt on it!" shouted Mary. "When the salt goes red you can Hoover it up … it'll be fine … trust me!"

"Trust me! Me arse, you silly bitch!" screamed Agnes, the hysterical hostess.

"Ah relax lovie, sure, sure Mary isn't used to them heavy John Roches glasses, 'twas an accident lovie. It isn't her fault she has a limp wrist," said John the hair dresser, Mary's husband.

"Who's on white?" inquired Richard.

"Me!"… "Me" … "Me" …

"Okay!' shouted Richard. "On the count of three, throw your white wine on the rug."

"Jesus Christ, Richard what are you doing?" screamed the still hysterical Agnes.

"One," cried Richard.

"Don't do it," screamed Agnes.

"Two," shouted Richard.

"You do this – and we're finished Richard!" shrieked Agnes.

Richard thought for a few seconds, took a deep breath and roared "Threeeeeeeeeeee …!"

The white wine splashed all over the rug, up the fireplace, on their shoes, over the skinny model, still lying there, unconscious. They couldn't believe their eyes. What had been a soggy red sheepskin rug, was now a pink soggier sheep skin rug.

"Now! That's more like the colour my uncle used on his sheep …."

"Oh shut up Sean!" they shouted.

Before their eyes, the sheepskin rug returned to its normal off-white sheepy color.

"Wow! That was like something magic," said John, his eyes all starry-like.

Richard glared at Agnes and said, "It's okay, I'm leaving!"

"But, but, no Richard, I didn't mean it … really …" pleaded Agnes.

"You can shag your rug for all I care!" barked Richard.

"Uhhh, now there's an idea" muttered Sean.

"Oh shut up Sean!" they shouted

Richard picked up the skinny model, threw her over his shoulder and left.

23. Why don't sharks eat sharks? Professional courtesy.

24. There are more chickens than people in the world.

FOR

.... I always find it's getting harder and harder to impress people when it comes to dinner parties. Gone are the days of Darina Allen-style cooking – lashings of butter, oceans of cream and large lumps of lard. When people come to dinner nowadays they want to know the fat content, how many points to each course. "Oh I must watch my weight" ... "It's okay, we watch it everytime we see you! and "Does my bum look big in this?" The answer is ... yes, it does you big fat cow! But you can't sat that so you always say, That's a lovely colour on you ... very slimming ... is it new? Your granny must have no curtains left, trying to cover an arse that size ...

So here's a simple recipe for a pavlova, laced with sugar, eggs, and large dollops of cream, and oh yes, the healthy part, fruit! Normally if you place the pavlova on the counter top so everybody can see it when they arrive, it's always a show stopper, and definite conversation starter, especially if it's the man who has made it. "Oh my god, that looks truly sinful" ... "Not at all, it's just a fresh fruit salad with a bit of meringue on the side."

Sometimes I have it strategically placed on the stairs when they arrive, so they can see it when they put their coats on the banisters. Then I move it around the house, just to tantalize and titillate their taste buds. It also means you don't have to worry too much about the main course, because by the time they sit down to dinner all they'll want to do is take their clothes off and jump naked into the creamy pavlova.

Oops, there goes the door bell again ... I'll be back

in a tick …

(about 15 minutes later)

sorry about that, it was the man from the parish wanting money for the new roof on the church. "Sure what nicer idea than an open air Mass," I said … He wasn't amused. I visited the Vatican two years ago, and the roof on St Peter's Basilica was big enough to cover all of Ireland … I exaggerate … okay Louth! Is it just me or is everyone looking for money these days. Anyway, where was I? Oh yes, the pavlova recipe, what you'll need is:

Pavlova

4 egg whites

get a dozen eggs, because 4 out of 12 successful egg separations is a good average

4oz of caster sugar
4oz of icing sugar
2 teaspoons of cornflour
1 teaspoon of white vinegar

A pinch of salt
8 fl oz of cream

in fact loads of cream. What ever is left over you can use for some party games later in the night, or if it's a boring party stick the cream on the Irish coffee.

One Cadbury's Flake	
Strawberries and kiwi fruit to decorate	
Electric beater	use different attachments for party games later
A baking tray	
A sieve	
Some parchment paper	you used it as tracing paper when you were in school
An oven	
A hammer	
A rubber spatula	can also be used for party games later in the night
A bottle of wine	this has nothing to do with the pavlova, it's just for you

Preheat oven to 160°C or gas mark 2-3. Line the baking tray with parchment paper.

Take a good sip of wine and congratulate yourself on separating the yokes from the egg whites. Place the egg whites and the pinch of salt into a large clean mixing bowl. Using the electric beater, beat the eggs gently until they get foamy. When the foam forms stiff peaks, take a sip of wine and enjoy. Add the two sugars gradually, beating constantly after each addition, until the mixture is thick and glossy and the sugar has dissolved.

Take another sip of wine, then using a metal spoon fold in the sifted cornflour and vinegar. Spoon the mixture onto the baking sheet, and using the spatula spread it around until it is 1 inch high all around. Bake in the oven for 45 minutes.

Take a sip of wine, peel the kiwis and slice into half moon shapes, wash and slice the strawberries, smash chocolate Flake with hammer while still in the packet. Finish off the wine, then take the pavlova out of the oven when cooked, and while still warm, place it onto a plate, peel off parchment paper, and leave to cool. Whip the cream, and spread it, fondly, onto the pavlova, and decorate with the kiwis and strawberries and Flake, and hey presto, one bottle of wine and 12 eggs later, you have a pavlova to be proud of!

Well done! Now get the playroom ready for the party games.

LASER

CHAPTER TWO

(Continued ...)

It was a glorious sunny day in Ireland, the smell of suntan lotion wafted through the nation ... no, it wasn't, it was raining, raining large buckets of water and there was an overwhelming pong of mould in the air, everybody was wet, damn wet!

Later that day Mary, no, a wet mouldy Mary, sank slowly into the psychiatrist's chair...

"What seems to be the problem?" asked the slightly damp shrink.

"If I knew that, I wouldn't be here!" barked Mary.

26. Winston Churchill was born in a Ladies Room.

25. All of the clocks in the movie "Pulp Fiction" are stuck on 4.20.

SURGERY

27. A cat has 32 muscles in each ear.

28. An ostrich's eye is bigger than its brain.

CHAPTER NINE

The Dictator

Batty was a dictator of a small island in the middle of the Atlantic Ocean. He had learnt everything there was to learn, from the island's previous dictator, JC …or CJ as he was known to his creditors. Batty loved to jog, drink, and socialize with world leaders, but his greatest failing was for blonde women. He loved blonde women, all types – big ones small ones, fat ones, and thin ones. He even had a favorite blonde joke written into the island's Constitution. It was the national joke: "Two blondes walked into a building – Jesus, you'd think one of them would have seen it!'

In the eyes of the island's peasants Batty could do nothing wrong.

"I'll ah raise de taxes!" he stuttered.

"Hooray! Hooray!" cried the peasants.

"I will never lie or tell de truth!" he claimed.

"Hooray to Honesty," cried the peasants.

"You shall have no health service, I will murder you all!" he declared.

"Hooray, we love you, Batty. We do, we love you, Batty we do!" they sang (off-key).

Batty was at the height of his popularity with the peasant population. There was even talk of him doing open-air concerts in stadiums, which would be specially built for him around the island. What would happen at these concerts was still a mystery, but his advisors, two thousand eight hundred and ten of them, were sure they could make something up.

It was a normal day for the island – peasants dying on the streets, blonde women running naked and free through department stores, and the dogs on the street prophesizing "the end is nigh' and then getting shot!

It was Monday, Batty was sitting in his solid gold suit, in his solid gold chair, in his solid gold office, listening to his language tapes. He was learning English. Suddenly there was a knock on the solid gold door.

"Who is it?" he shouted.

"It's me!" came the reply.

"Who's me?" he shouted back.

"Ah …Batty?!" said Mr. Slightly Confused from behind the golden door.

"Sure I'm Batty. How can you be me when I'm me!" said the great dictator.

"No no, you don't understand, I'm not saying I'm you, I just said it's me …," said the stranger, hesitantly.

"Yah I heard ya de first time, I'm not tick ya know, but you did say you were me?" questioned Batty.

"No I said …, look, can I just come in, please. I've something really important to tell you," he said still behind the closed golden door.

"Okay, in you come, but you'd better not be me or I'll have you shot!" said Batty the great.

The golden door swung open, and in walked this incredible specimen of a man – tall, broad shoulders, perfect skin, sparkling eyes, muscles bulging from under his shirt and an exotic aroma that would make Batty's blondes wilt.

" Ah hah, I was right, you're not me at all!" cheered Batty.

"DAD!" announced the tearful stranger.

"Son?" said a very surprised Batty.

"Yes …dad …I'm your son, your only son," he began to weep…

"SON!" choked Batty.

"DAD …DEE!" cried his son.

"But …but …you can't be," said a breathless Batty.

"Oh but I am, dad," he said, with his arms outstretched, waiting for a fatherly hug.

"But, you're big!" stuttered Batty. "You're bulging, you're

…beautiful …" stammered Batty.

"Just like my father!" cried his son.

"But, but … you're black!' cried an amazed Batty.

When Batty was a student he went to America to study accountancy. He failed, but that didn't stop him having a good time. It wasn't long before he ran out of money, so he was reduced to drastic measures. He sold his sperm. At that time there was a shortage of white Irish male sperm in America. Batty quite enjoyed his daily trip to the sperm bank – all it took was two pages of a soft porn magazine *(National Geographic)* and his cup was full, *(teaspoon more like – according to a reliable source).*

By some strange coincidence his sperm was chosen by an Asian woman, because she always liked the idea of having a bit of Irish in her.

"Call security, dere's a refugee in my office," he shouted at his intercom.

"I'm not a refugee. I'm your son, Zachary. I'm a professor of English in Harvard University. I'm only here finding my roots," he claimed.

"The only root your going to get is up de hole …security! Security! Where is the damn security?" shouted Batty, banging the intercom with his fist.

Zachary tried to calm him down. "I assure you I'm your son, I know we don't share the same skin colour, but …"

"But nothing!" shouted batty. "It's not your skin that's the problem. It's your damn hair! It's RED!"

The golden door burst open, the Minister for Internal Security, Macky Mac, stood there frozen. He suffered from a rare condition only known to the islanders – the 'Gruaige Dearg' complex. You see, only people with black hair and freckles were allowed on the island, and the sight of a red-haired person made Macky Mac go all strange like. It made his body go into spasm, first a frozen-like state, followed by heavy sweating, culminating in a violent rush of adrenaline through his veins, turning his skin green, trebling the size of his muscles, forcing him to burst out of his clothes. *[This was normally accompanied by strange music playing in the background.]*

"GGGRRRRRRR …" growled the half-naked Minister for Internal Security. His trousers, though tight, always managed to stay on.

"But father you can't to this to me, I'm your son, your own flesh and blood!" Zachary pleaded, with his arms still outstretched, waiting for a fatherly hug. "I'll shave my head!" he pleaded.

"It'll grow back. It always grows back!" snarled Batty.

"Okay, okay …I'll dye it red!" he cried.

"No, no, you'd look silly! And anyways, it's too late for that now!" said Batty, with a tinge of sadness in his voice.

"…RRRRRRRRRRRRRRRR …" roared the Minister. It's all he could say due to the large swelling in his tonsils.

Batty ran to the window, and opened the large golden lock.

"Quick Macky, fire him through de window!" Batty shouted. The Minister grabbed Zachary and held him high over his head, spinning him around and around like an aeroplane propeller ready for take-off.

"On de count of three Macky …one …two …three …FIRE!" screeched Batty.

"Ooohhhhhhhhh …Ffffuuuuuuuuuuuuuuuuuuuuu …" were the last words that were heard from Zachary, as he was hurled through the window, over the city, over the mountains, splashing into the sea somewhere outside the twelve mile city limit.

Batty calmly closed the window, fixed his tie, and sat back into his golden chair, then he looked at his Minister for Internal Security and said, "Listen here, Macky, we're going to have to do something about your clothes allowance!"

Years past, Zackary didn't write and Batty didn't reply.

The Slither Party

You will need:

4 metres of heavy-duty gardening plastic

A scissors

A roll of strong gaffer tape

8 large containers of baby oil

Lay the plastic on the floor, making sure it goes about 4 inches up the wall. Seal it onto the wall with the gaffer tape, also seal any gaps in the plastic with the gaffer tape. Take 7 containers of baby oil [leave the other one till later] and spread liberally around the room. Turn on the heating and dim the lights, leave to settle while you're having your dinner, then after your guests have taken their clothes off and jumped naked into your pavlova, you can move into the playroom for a slither party. The games you play are at your own discretion, but Twister is always a favourite ... Enjoy!

29. The giant squid has the largest eyes in the world.

30. The microwave was invented after a researcher walked by a radar tube, and the bar of chocolate in his pocket melted.

I've decided to grow a beard for this project, I thought it might give me more muse! But now I realise I need more than a beard to help me, maybe a storyline would help … here, let's try this …

CHAPTER TEN

The sun was setting on the horizon, beams of light shone through the breaks in the luminous red clouds, it was like Jesus was about to appear through the clouds and say "…

*So what do you think he said, cause I haven't a clue …
I've got to go have some dinner, tonight it's Colette's
Fishy Dishy … hmmmmm tasty …*

31. A dentist invented the electric chair.

32. John Lennon's first girlfriend was named Thelma Pickles.

The man with the oil paintings called today, the paintings are absolutely awful. I don't understand how anybody in their right mind would buy such rubbish, yet every time he calls we are always so polite. "We're just doing up the house at the moment, so maybe if you call again in two months, we might have a better idea where we'd put them." ...

Instead we should say "they're shite, they're shite now, they were shite two months ago, and they'll still be shite two months from now, we hate oil paintings! Now go away!"

... I wonder would that work ...

33. There are 336 dimples on a regulation golf ball.

34. A gold fish has a memory span of 3 seconds.

... after making the pavlova you will have a load of left over yokes (egg yokes that is) so what can we do with them? Throw them out? No, cause they will leak. Throw them in a plastic bag. No, cause they will stink your bin. Drink them? No, that would be disgusting. Pour them down the sink? You could do that but that would be a waste, think off all the starving children in the world. Put them in sealed tubberware container and send them to Africa? No, that would be silly, so what I suggest we do is make Some Ice Cream, yes Some Ice Cream.

BB's Crunchy Ice Cream.

You will need:

4 yokes

6oz caster sugar

8 fun size 'crunchies'

1 pint of cream (if you want it in litres look up a cookery book!)

2 glasses of wine (you should be quite thirsty by now)

First take a sip of wine, then using an electric beater, whip the yolks and the caster sugar together until the mixture is thick and pale (like your average Irish man). Take another sip of wine.

Place the 'crunchies' in a plastic bag, and hammer the living day lights out of them. Finish the glass of wine because that was quite energetic.

Whip the cream until it forms stiff peaks but no to stiff. Pour a second glass of wine. Then fold the egg yolk mixture, the smashed 'crunchies' and the cream together.

Pour into a suitable container and place in the freezer for two hours. Finish your glass of wine.

Ice cream tips:

Always cover the surface of your ice cream with baking paper or cling wrap. This will stop ice crystals forming on the top. For full flavour, never eat your ice cream rock hard, always eat it slightly soft!

(Pervert!)

Suitable for 6 month to 18 month olds only.

What does the cow say?
MOOOOOO

What does the chicken say?
BOK BOK BOK BOK

What does the cat say? MEOW
MEOW MEOW

What does the dog say? RUFF
RUFF RUFF RUFF

What does the sheep say? BA
BA BA BAAAA

What does the pig say? HAVE
YOU BEEN DRINKING, STEP OUT
OF THE VEHICLE AND BLOW INTO
THIS!

What does the fat pig say?
I'M WRECKED, I NEED TO SIT
DOWN.

What does the donkey say? HE
HAW HE HAW HE HAWWWW

36. A kangaroo can jump up to thirty feet.

35. The longest word in the English language is "pneumonoultramicroscopicsilicovolcanoconiosis". It's a lung disease caused by breathing in volcanic particles.

ENDING ONE

The Book – At Last

I managed to make my way to the road and hitch a lift. Two old dears in a blue Starlet on a Sunday drive, 25mph in the fast lane, I would have been quicker jumping on Frisky's back. They dropped me to the Hawk's Hotel, a favourite lunchtime spot with my wife, Linda. I walked into the lobby and was greeted by the manager, Bob.

"How ya, looks like you had a good night," he laughed.

"Don't talk to me …," I said. He came closer and whispered into my ear, "you know there's no dogs allowed."

"So how did your wife get in?" I said half jokingly, and I mean only half, you should have seen her, so Bob politely escorted Frisky off the premises. "Oh speaking of wives, yours is in the bar," he said, tripping over Frisky's tail.

I looked into the bar, and there was my wife sitting with a man I recognized, yet I couldn't place him. They were deep in conversation. She had a worried look on her face. He had his arms around her, as if consoling her in some way. I decided I'd order a taxi and go the Garda station, less fuss than bringing them to me, and it would save me having to explain the situation to Bob. I went to reception to order a taxi.

"Oh Mr. Reilly, we weren't expecting you today, what can I do for you?" said the concierge. I'd never seen him before, I thought it strange that he knew who I was.

"A taxi please, as soon as you can, tell them I'll be waiting outside."

Two minutes later a car pulled up with a jerk, the jerk got out, I got in *(the old ones are the best)*.

"Garda station, and make it quick," I said.

"No problem, Mr. Reilly," said the driver.

"Sorry, but how do you know my name?" I enquired.

"Oh I know more than your name, I know your wife has a tattoo on her left buttock, and I know you're supposed to be dead!" He turned his head to look at me. It was the man from the bar with my wife. "And now I'm going to finish what my morons failed to finish last night!" he shouted.

I tried to get out of the car. The doors were locked. He revved up the engine. Just as he released the hand brake, a dog jumped onto the bonnet, barking and snarling at the driver: Frisky, coming to my rescue one more time. With his attention taken by Frisky, I grabbed him by the throat. He put his foot on the accelerator and the car took off across the car park. Frisky was flung onto the roof and rolled off the boot, and gave a loud painful whine. We struggled for control of the wheel. We were heading straight for a car, when with all my might I punched him in the face, breaking his jaw in the process. Blood and teeth spattered across the side window. I jumped back and managed to fasten my safety belt before the car crashed, catapulting the driver through the windscreen and into the back seat of the other car. I slowly pulled myself out of the car, and approached the driver's legs which were sticking out of a blue Starlet, the old dears' Starlet. He was dead. My wife came running across the car park, shouting "you're alive, you're alive!" and trying to hide her disappointment.

She got life in jail, Frisky lost a leg, and from there on the old dears used their free transport on the bus.

37. The longest moustache in the world is over 8 feet long.

ENDING TWO

The Book – At Last

I knew my wife was having an affair with a drug dealer, but I never thought she'd have me killed, or maybe she didn't, and he just wanted her money, our money. First he got my wife and then he got me, well, that's what he thought. The only way into his ranch was by air. He lived in a 20-acre farm in Kildare, surrounded by high security fencing, guards and killer dogs.

I took a parachuting lesson. The first half of the day was spent jumping off chairs, shouting, "one thousand, two thousand, three thousand, four thousand, lines, canopy, clear!"

In the afternoon, three of us piled into the one-seater plane, it sounded like a flying lawnmower, three grown men kneeling down on all fours with their face in each other's arse, hoping to God none of them would fart. The first two jumped, hesitantly, then it was my turn. I grabbed a nail file from inside my sock, and held it to the pilot's throat. "Fly me to Straffan!" I shouted.

"What the fu …" he muttered.

"Fly me to Straffan, or this plane goes down, and there's only one parachute, and its on my back!" I shouted.

"But we don't have enough fuel to get there and back," he pleaded.

"I don't want to come back!"

I smiled as he turned the plane in the right direction, and when we were over the ranch, I stepped out onto the wing, my heart pounding louder than the noise from the plane, and jumped. Somehow the jumping from the chair was much easier. The plane flew away into the distance, and as I sailed effortlessly through the air, my peace was disturbed by the sound of the plane's engine running out of fuel, as it glided down motorway creating a two-mile pile-up.

I landed safely in the horse's stables. I released myself from my parachute, and skulked around to find my wife, and the men who had tried to kill me. By the time I got to the house the police had arrived. There had been a report of the pilot jumping from the plane and landing close by. I was arrested for trespassing, and thrown into jail for two years. At least I was safe, and my cheating druggie wife didn't get a million euro. The parachute club was closed down.

ENDING THREE

The Book – At Last

Myself and Frisky headed for home. Frisky kept barking at me. "What is it, Frisky?" I said, he barked some more. "There's a boy trapped down a well. Where?" I asked. He barked some more. "Okay, Frisky, we'd better go help!" So we ran to the old well, and as we approached we could the faint sounds of "help help!"

I've had enough of this rubbish. If you want to finish it, please be my guest. If you want to write another ending, please fire away, or if you'd like to tell us which ending you preferred, please e-mail us at publishing@merlin.ie

38. If you stretched out your intestines, they'd be about 25 feet long.

39. The fourth funnel on the *Titanic* was built for show. It was thought the more funnels a ship had, the faster it would go.

The End

At last. I couldn't wait for this bit cause my back is slouched, my shoulders are killing me, my wrists are paining, and my fingers are all overee thetttt plaieceece. I'm tired.

Goodbye now and thanks for reading. And before I go I'd like to thank the man or woman who invented spell-check. It's feckin' great!